Dumbo

Starring

Mrs Jumbo

Timothy

First published by Parragon in 2010

Parragon
Queen Street House
4 Queen Street
Bath BA1 1HE, UK

ISBN 978-1-4075-8452-2

Printed in China

Disney

DUMBO

Bath · New York · Singapore · Hong Kong · Cologne · Delhi · Melbourne

Mr Stork flew down and landed on the roof of a train car. "Oh, Mrs Jumbo! Special delivery for Mrs Jumbo!" he called, hopping from one train car to the next.

From one car, Mr Stork saw several elephant trunks waving at him. Mr Stork hopped into the train car. "Which one of you ladies is expecting a little bundle of joy?" he asked.

"Right over there," the elephants answered, pointing to Mrs Jumbo. Everyone cooed when the bundle fell open.

"Aaachoo!" the little elephant sneezed. His ears, which had been neatly tucked behind his head, flopped open. They were enormous!

The elephants shrieked with laughter. "Just look at those ears," one elephant giggled. "Why, with those ears, you should call him 'Dumbo!'"

The elephants' teasing made Mrs Jumbo angry. Turning her back on the others, she picked up her baby, carried him to a corner of the train car and lay down beside him.

She didn't care if her baby's ears were big. She thought he was beautiful just the way he was. Cuddling him in her trunk, she gently rocked him to sleep.

The next day, the townspeople followed the parade to the circus ground.

"Hurry, hurry, hurry! Step right up and get your tickets!" The circus barker called to the gathering crowd.

Inside the elephant tent, Mrs Jumbo was quietly bathing Dumbo when a bunch of rowdy boys ran in.

"Look at those ears!" they shouted when they saw Dumbo.
"Isn't that the funniest thing you ever saw?" The boys
wiggled their ears and stuck out their tongues at Dumbo.
Laughing and jeering, the boys pulled Dumbo's ears.
Mrs Jumbo wanted to protect her baby. She picked up a
bale of straw and threw it at the boys to scare them away.
"Help! Mad elephant!" they screamed.

10

The Ringmaster dashed into the tent. "Down, Mrs Jumbo!" he shouted, cracking his whip in the air.

Then someone tried to pull Dumbo away. Furious, Mrs Jumbo bellowed and charged.

"Lock her up," the Ringmaster commanded.

As Dumbo watched, the trainers dragged his mother away. They locked her in a wagon that was set apart from the rest of the circus. There, with her legs in chains, Mrs Jumbo stood alone, weeping for her baby.

Dumbo, crying for his mother, thought he had no friends in the world as the other elephants turned their back on him.

But Dumbo was wrong. Someone did want to be his friend.

In a corner of the tent sat a little mouse named Timothy. He had seen and heard everything. When Timothy saw how the other elephants treated Dumbo, it made him mad.

"Look at that poor little fella," the little mouse said. "Everyone's making fun of his ears. What's the matter with them? I think they're cute."

"Aw, you aren't afraid of little old me, are you?" Timothy asked Dumbo, who was hiding. "I'm Timothy Mouse and I'm your friend, Dumbo. I have a plan to help you free your mother."

At that, Dumbo forgot all about being scared.

"I know you're embarrassed by your ears, kid," Timothy said. "But lots of people with big ears are famous. So all we gotta do is make you a big star. But first we need a really colossal act. And I'm just the fellow to think of one. Leave everything to me."

The next day, Timothy had put his plan to make Dumbo a star into action. The Ringmaster blew his whistle, and the first elephant climbed on top of a large ball.

Dumbo and Timothy watched as the pyramid rose higher and higher, until it almost reached the top of the tent.

"And now, Ladies and Gentlemen," the Ringmaster shouted, "the world's smallest elephant will spring to the top of the pyramid!"

But before Dumbo could make his leap, his ears became untied and he stumbled over them, right into the elephant pyramid.

For a moment, the stunned crowd watched in silence as the elephant pyramid teetered and swayed. Then they ran for their lives as the elephants began to fall.

Trumpeting and bellowing, the elephants tumbled down, crashing into beams and platforms and bleachers. They smacked into walls and pulled down wires and ropes. Finally, they crashed into the centre tent pole.

The enormous tent began to sway and billow.

Then, with a huge groan, it collapsed. Dumbo was left sitting alone and forlorn in the middle of the ruins.

The very next show, the clowns painted Dumbo's face and
dressed him as a baby. They put him on a tiny platform high
up in a building surrounded by crackling, make-believe flames.
Dumbo stood shaking with fear, while far below, clowns
dressed as firemen ran around squirting hoses at each other.

"The baby will have to jump!" a clown fireman announced. The rest of the firemen held up a thin safety net.

Closing his eyes, Dumbo leaped from the building. Dumbo fell through the net and landed in a tub of wet plaster. The audience roared with laughter.

As the clowns bowed to the cheering crowds, they paid no attention to Dumbo, who crept from the tent feeling hurt, humiliated and miserable.

After the show, the clowns celebrated in their tent. "Cheer up, Dumbo," Timothy said as he scrubbed his friend's sad little face.

"I've found out where they're keeping your mother. I'm going to take you to see her later tonight."

A wistful smile crossed Dumbo's face. Things wouldn't seem so bad if he could just see his mother.

Later that night, while most of the circus folk slept, Timothy took Dumbo
to the wagon where his mother was chained. "Mrs Jumbo, someone to see you!"
Timothy called.

Mrs Jumbo put her trunk through the bars of the window and stroked Dumbo's
head. She wrapped her trunk around Dumbo and rocked him lovingly.

At last it was time to leave. Tearfully, Dumbo and his mother waved goodbye.

As Timothy and Dumbo returned to the clowns' tent, they heard the clowns talking about their act. "Let's make the house taller tomorrow," shouted a clown.

Dumbo felt sad, he didn't like being laughed at by so many people during the clown's act, and a taller house just sounded scary.

All Dumbo wanted was to be with his mother. He started to cry. Dumbo was tired. Timothy sat by his side and tried to comfort Dumbo. As Dumbo stopped crying he eyes began to droop until finally they were shut tight. And as Dumbo fell asleep he started to have the strangest dream...

As dawn broke, a flock of crows perched on a tall tree stared at the strangest sight they'd ever seen.

There on a branch, high above the ground, a little elephant lay sleeping peacefully. And in his trunk was a mouse. It was Dumbo and Timothy.

"We'd better wake those two up and find out what they're doing here," the crows decided. "This is our tree. Elephants don't belong up here."

Dumbo woke so fast, he fell out of the tree. The crows laughed. "Aw, don't pay any attention to them," Timothy said, helping Dumbo up. "I do wonder how we got up in that tree, though."

"Maybe you flew!" one of the crows shouted.

"Oh, sure." Timothy shrugged his shoulders. "Maybe we –"
Timothy stopped and stared at Dumbo's ears. "That's it, Dumbo!"
he exclaimed. "Your ears! They're perfect wings! You're the world's
only flying elephant!"

The crows started laughing at Dumbo.

"You should be ashamed, picking on a little fella like that!"
Timothy scolded them.

The crows felt bad. One of them handed Timothy a black feather. "Tell him this is a magic feather," he said, "and so long as he holds onto it, he can fly."

Timothy gave Dumbo the feather and told him what the crows had said. Dumbo believed every word. "Now all we need is a little flying practice," Timothy said, climbing into Dumbo's hat.

Dumbo clutched his feather, closed his eyes, flapped his ears and suddenly he was soaring. The crows flew alongside the little elephant, cheering him on. "Why, he flies just like an eagle. Better than an aeroplane!" they crowed.

"Hot diggity! You're flying! You're really flying!" Timothy shouted. "I knew you could do it! Wait till the next performance. We'll show everyone what you can do!"

Soon it was time for Dumbo to perform again with the clowns. He stood on the platform with Timothy perched on his trunk. The clowns had built the burning house higher, and the ground looked very, very far away.

But this time Dumbo wasn't afraid.

He clutched his magic feather in his trunk and waited for his cue.

"Come on, jump! Jump!" the clowns shouted.

"Boy, are they in for a surprise!" Timothy chuckled as Dumbo jumped from the platform. But as they flew through the air, the wind tore the feather from Dumbo's trunk. Dumbo froze. Without his magic feather, he didn't believe he could fly. He and Timothy hurtled towards the ground.

Timothy slid to the end of Dumbo's trunk. "Open your ears and fly!" he pleaded. "The magic feather was just a gag. You can fly all by yourself!"

Dumbo heard Timothy's words and believed them. And what's
more, he believed in himself. At the last second, Dumbo spread
his ears, soaring up and up and up.

The astonished audience went wild as Dumbo zoomed after the
clowns, chasing them around the ring. The crowd roared as he
dove at the Ringmaster. They applauded thunderously as Dumbo
did loop-the-loops and rolls and spins in the air.

27

Dumbo was famous. All the newspapers carried pictures of him and Timothy. Most importantly, Mrs Jumbo was let out of her cage, because the Ringmaster was so pleased with Dumbo.

Dumbo thought it was great fun being a star. But what he loved best of all…was being with his mother once again.

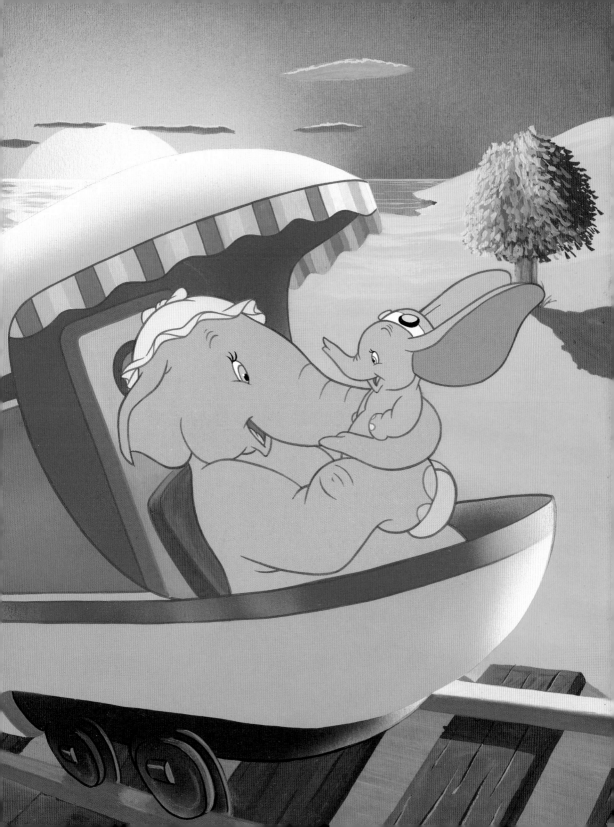